I0626336

Stolen
to
Oz

Toto and Miss Jennie
in Oz
without Dorothy

Other books by Alan Lindsay (Alanglindsay.com)
Ambaguam, Beginning at the End
A, a novel
The Burzee Rose, a Christmas Carol

by Alan Lindsay and Dennis Anfuso
OzHouse
OzHouse Reopened: The Curse of Budistiltskin

by Dennis Anfuso (DennisAnfuso.com)
The Winged Monkeys of Oz
The Astonishing Tale of the Gump of Oz
A Promise Kept in Oz

Forthcoming by Alan Lindsay and Dennis Anfuso
Intruder in the Realm

Stolen to Oz

Toto and Miss Jennie
in Oz
(without Dorothy)

Alan Lindsay

Interset
Press

2020

Stolen to Oz: Toto and Miss Jennie in Oz without Dorothy by Alan Lindsay
Illustrations by Dennis Anfuso
Text Copyright © 2020 by Alan Lindsay
   All rights reserved. No part of this book may be reproduced or transmitted in any form or by any means, electronic or mechanical, including photocopying, recording, scanning, or by any information storage and retrieval system, including the Internet and the World Wide Web, without permission from the Publisher, except in the case of brief quotations embodied in critical articles and reviews.
   This is a work of fiction. Any resemblance of characters in this book to actual persons, living or dead, is unintentional and purely coincidental.
   9 8 7 6 5 4 3 2 1 /0 1
Interset Press
35 Burns Hill Road
Wilton, New Hampshire 03086
Interset Press is a registered trademark and "Fiddler," the Interset Press colophon, is a trademark of Linda Anfuso.
Book design by Geimle Burzeen.
Cover Art by Dan Fuso
Cover Design by Sarah Jean Lindsay
Many thanks to Tom Benson and Cathy Lindsay for their proofreading prowess.
Printed in the United States of America. First Interset Press edition: June 2020
Library of Congress Cataloguing-in-Publication Data: Lindsay, Alan
Stolen to Oz: Toto and Miss Jennie in Oz without Dorothy
Summary: Jennie Grierson, Dr. Morgan Fiddledog and Toto are lured by a stray hot air balloon to the magical land of Oz.
[1. Fantasy. 2. Fairytales. 3. Oz. 4. Lindsay, Alan 5. Anfuso, Dennis] 1. Title [Fic.]
   ISBN: 978-1-57433-049-6

for Sarah

1

Miss Jennie Grierson lived up the road from the Gales. She had a nice piece of land and a big old house that used to be a plantation house. It was not in the best repair, but it was holding up all right, considering how long it had been since there had been a plantation there. Now there was only a farm. At least she called it a farm. Claire, her niece, called it a garden. Whatever it was, it was hers and she was holding on to it.

And she was lucky to be doing it, too. The cyclone had knocked down houses all over the area. The Gales' house was carried clear away by the huge funnel cloud with their girl Dorothy in it. Dorothy came back under mysterious circumstances. But the house was never seen again. They'd begun the long, slow process of replacing it. Miss Jennie could hear the sound of the saws and hammers when the wind was right.

Miss Jennie's house survived without a scratch, although she herself had not fared as well. She'd been on her way to town on her bicycle when the storm hit. Some people thought she was too old to ride a bike—Claire certainly did. But lots of women in Potawatomie Country rode bikes, and some of them were older than she was. And she was not going to listen to anyone tell her she could not ride a bike to town and put some groceries in her basket, and ride home whenever she chose.

She had to admit that bike riding on that particular day had not been wise. But who could have known? The funnel cloud came up from nowhere—completely without warning. And it came from

behind her, and it sounded like the train. It was almost upon her when she turned around and saw it racing in her direction like a wild animal—like she was a little mouse and it was an overgrown coyote set to pounce. She pumped her old dancer's legs as fast as they would go. The roaring wind tugged at the pins in her hat and made her dress flap against the tires of her bike. But she was strong, and she was fast, and she was sure she'd make it to where the wind could do her no harm.

And she would have made it too, without a scratch—if that large tree hadn't cracked with a sound like a gun exploding right beside her. It thumped to the ground so hard she could swear it made her bike jump clear off the road. Once the bike was airborne, her pumping legs were useless. The wind tipped her onto the ground with just a flick of its paw.

But she was okay. Maybe she was no longer what they called a spring chicken, but she was still spry enough. She even managed to swing her leg clear the of the bike as it was falling over and do a kind of pirouette—the first she'd done in more than thirty years— before she collapsed on the ground, hitting a rock—but it wasn't a very big rock—with her right knee.

By then the cyclone had moved a safe distance away, in the direction of the Gale farm. It didn't appear as though it would make the turn to her place, so that was okay. The wind where she fell had already died down to where it was no longer a threat even to the security of her hat.

She rubbed her knee. It would probably be swollen up pretty good tomorrow, she thought. But she'd gotten used to injuries like that back in her dancing days. It was nothing to worry about.

The same could not be said for her beautiful bike. The front wheel was bent and so were the forks. It was unrideable. She dragged it a few hundred yards. But by then her knee hurt pretty bad. She left it by a tree for Claire to come get after the storm passed.

She was very surprised, a few days later, to hear how much damage the Gale farm had received and that Dorothy (a very wild child who lacked the good sense to get herself into the storm cellar) had been carried away along with her dog.

Nature had a way of clearing the decks of certain types of people, she told Claire.

She first realized Dorothy must have somehow made it back home when her little dog showed at the Grierson farm. Miss Jennie was sitting on the front porch because the day was hot, shucking peas. And that little black dog walked right up her front steps and yipped. (The dog was as wild as the little girl and free to roam wherever it wanted now that the Gales' fence was all beaten down and the new house was yet without windows or doors.)

"Shoo," she said, "get on home."

Jennie hated dogs. She hated almost all animals, even horses. They were smelly and dirty, and they were either demanding or poorly trained, every one of them. That's why she rode a bike.

"Get out of my yard," she said, kicking at the little beast, almost spilling her bowl of peas. But the dog kept barking as though it wanted her to follow it.

"Where're you thinking you're gonna get me to go? Unless you're a banker and you're leading me to a pot of gold, I have no interest in trailing you. Now you get home."

She finally managed to chase it away with a broom.

She told Claire about it, but Claire just rolled her eyes. Claire wasn't talking to her any more than she had to, not since Miss Jennie had told her she absolutely was *not* going to pay for her to go to some dead-end art institute in New York City. Yes, she'd promised her brother before he died that she'd put the money he'd left behind toward her education. But when she said that, she meant she'd use it for something a good deal more practical than art school. A good agricultural college, a good business school. This house she lived in was going to be her house one day, and she'd have to learn to take care of it. And furthermore, she had a proud, old name in this town, and this was where she belonged.

Dorothy's little dog returned the next day, and again she chased it home with a broom, warning it never to come back. Maybe the dog was trying to tell her that Dorothy needed help, Claire suggested. If so, Miss Jennie let her know, she had her own people to help her just fine. Claire said, "You might try being nice for once."

Imagine an orphan accusing the aunt that has raised her from a little girl to an adult, spending her own money (mostly) with hardly any help from anyone, of not being nice?

Jennie bit her tongue.

On the third day when the dog returned again, Jennie decided she was going to do something about it. She got a big net with a long handle out of the barn. And she scooped that dog up like it was a butterfly. She did it so deftly the little creature was in the net before it knew what was coming. And then she took the net and upturned it into her bike basket. (The dog tried to bite her once or twice, and in fact did manage to give her a little nip on the end of her finger. But that was all it could manage. It was nice to still have such sharp reflexes at her age.) She locked the basket shut and tied it onto her newly repaired bike—and she headed into town.

It wouldn't do any good to give the dog back to the Gales. It would just run away again. She was going to take it to downtown Wamego and let it go on the street, or maybe behind the drug store where no one would see. Let it try to find its way home from there—the ugly little beast!

15

2

Miss Jennie Grierson always knew where she was, and she always paid attention to where she was going.

The same cannot be said of Doctor Morgan Fiddledog and his traveling sideshow. On the flat, straight roads of Kansas, the doctor was apt to put his horse in charge of the driving while he napped or fiddled on the seat or even slipped into the back for a bite and a nip. Sometimes, as the driverless wagon clopped down the long, empty backroads of Potawatomie county, he slipped into the back out of the sun and pulled out his fiddle and worked his way through his whole repertoire just for fun. And that's what he was doing when Miss Jennie Grierson, from what was probably a mile away, laid eyes on the faded circus wagon ambling toward her, taking up both sides of the road.

She had plenty of time to avoid a collision. And the plodding horse had plenty of time to get out of her way. There was not a reason in the world why a mishap should happen.

To make safe navigation all the more certain, Miss Jennie took to yelling and then screaming at the vehicle before she was within a half mile of it, calling it dreadful names and telling it which side of the road it was supposed to traveling down, according to the law.

She became all the more strident the moment she noticed that there was no one in the driver's seat.

The doctor in the back, singing and playing, filled the wagon with so much sound he did not hear Miss Jennie's self-righteous cries until she was almost upon him. That was when he stuck his head

out the front, just in time to see the old woman in the long dress veer off to the left at precisely the one place in the road where such a veering could create a problem: at the bridge over the stream where sometimes the doctor parked his show for the night.

Down she tumbled.

3

The doctor recognized her right away. He hadn't yet met her or even seen her in person. But everyone in Potawatomie County knew who Miss Jennie Grierson was. Her family was no longer what it had been in her grandfather's day, but her name or picture still appeared somewhere in the *Potawatomie Picayune* almost every day. Whether it was on a letter complaining about how the county needed to step up the enforcement of leash laws or as head (or chair or doyen) of some civic committee or business board entrusted with improving this or that aspect of the town, the county, or even sometimes the state, she was always there, and she always had something to say.

And she had it in for the doctor. She had already gone to her old family friend the sheriff to request that he drive the old man's "vagabond wagon and humbug side-show" out of the county.

The beleaguered sheriff had already pored over all the law books in his office trying to find in them something that would give him the authority to make this happen. And although he had not yet managed to find anything that would do the job, he had paid Doctor Fiddledog a visit, advising him that there would be no business for him around these parts "if he knew what was good for him."

What was good for him turned out to be something that the doctor did not know. And the part about there being "no business for him around these parts," that didn't turn out to be quite true either. The doctor had brought his wagon to a halt outside the General Store at the North End of Main Street in the town of Wamego two days in a row now. Drawing crowds was easy. All he did was park his wagon at the center of town, stand upon the seat, hoist his fiddle, and invigorate the public square with a rich array of barnyard airs. But though the people gathered to sing and sway, the entertainment brought him no coin. That came from sales. He did a steady business of palm reading, tea gazing, and phrenological assessments, as well as a reasonable trade in gums, ointments, and tonics. But what best filled his coffer was *Dr. Morgan's Magical Elixir*, which he sold in little green bottles of one dose each and which served to cure Rheumatism, Rheumatic Fever, Rhubarbery, Splenetic Porphyry, Systemic Lethargy, Choleric Effusion, and— the most troublesome malady of all—Rueful Veracity, which was a condition in which the sufferer, according to the label, "feels compelled by scruple to say more than does him good."

Rueful Veracity turned out to be a condition the sheriff himself suffered from. On the day of the lawman's visit, the doctor sold Sheriff Hafstripe half a dozen bottles.

How did the doctor know that the sheriff suffered from Rueful Veracity? In his conversation, the sheriff had let slip that the force directing him to remove the showman from the county was not the county law but the prominent owner of a rundown plantation some distance from town. The effect of this news was not to push the doctor from Pottawatomie County but to cause him rather to dig in his heels, to lead him perhaps to stay on in Wamego even slightly beyond the point at which it was profitable to do so. Miss Jennie Grierson would have called it "pure orneriness," but Doctor Morgan Fiddledog called it pride. Whatever it was called, the truth was he found women like Miss Grierson interesting, in a purely scientific way. And he liked a challenge.

Doctor Morgan Fiddledog suffered from a condition known as "Obstinate Sanguinity," which made him set about doing hard things cheerfully and giving people what was good for them whether they liked it or not. (Sadly, this condition was not improved by single doses of Dr. Morgan's Elixir but was known to respond to the application of several dozen.)

After the sheriff left, and while he was still counting his return on investment, the doctor did a little informal research on Miss Jennie Grierson.

The first thing he found was that, despite her prominence, no one in Potawatomie country seemed to like her very much. As far as he could tell, she didn't have any friends. (Folks were more likely to call her a witch than a friend.) Of course she must have had friends somewhere, but wherever they were, they did not walk the Main Street of Wamego. The second thing he learned is that she had almost no family. Her father, almost the last surviving member of her family besides herself, had passed on around twenty years ago; her mother had died ten years before that, and Jennie had never had a sister. She had had one brother who had died in the war, and that brother had had a daughter, named Claire, Jennie's only living relative, as far as anyone knew. Claire lived with her in the big, old house. But they'd had a falling out recently. Claire wanted to go to school in a big city and Jennie wouldn't let her. Claire even threatened to leave the farm and "make it on her own," and indeed had left once already to do just that. But the sheriff had found her and hauled her back home. Claire had to accept that because she was still legally a child. But she swore that on her eighteenth birthday, she would leave the old house for good, and there was nothing any aunt or any sheriff could do about it.

The clever, generous, optimistic doctor didn't know which Grierson to feel sorrier for.

The last thing the doctor learned about Miss Jennie was the most interesting thing of all. It put a new spin on everything else he'd heard. Years ago Jennie Grierson had been a dancer, a dancer of some talent. She'd specialized in ballet, but she did whatever kind of dancing could be done: waltz, Charleston, Two-Step, Grizzly Bear, Turkey Trot. You name it, she did it. She'd won contests. She'd performed in shows. And she'd had dreams of leaving Kansas to try out for the New York City Ballet, and everyone who knew her back then thought she would make it too.

But then her mother had died. And she had to take care of her father. And then her father died and she had to take care of what was left of the family's legacy. Back then she'd certainly had friends. In fact, she was popular, and everyone in the county was in her corner. They all wanted her to go to New York and put Pottawatomie on the map.

The doctor decided this was enough information for him to deal with Jennie Grierson, should their paths ever happen to cross, which they almost certainly would once she found out that he was in no hurry to leave the county.

So when he saw her tumble into the ditch beside the bridge his first impulse was to feel sorry for her. His second impulse was to laugh. His third impulse was to suppress his second impulse, which he did just in time, just before the laugh rising through his chest found its way to his lips.

21

Jennie swung her right leg back, up, and over the seat of the bike in a smooth athletic motion just as she had done when the cyclone had pushed her over, in a motion her body must certainly have remembered from her dancing days. Her left foot stayed firmly on the pedal of the bike even as the bike began to lean toward the ground. No circus performer could have managed the trick better. It appeared for just a moment that she'd execute a perfect pirouette off the bike, releasing the handlebars and leaping from the pedal to the ground, winding up gracefully *en pointe* as the bike and its basket came rattling to the ground. And she might have done it too, if she hadn't felt a sharp pain in her injured knee, which led to her dropping her leg just enough that her long dress caught on the seat and knocked her foot into the basket strapped behind it. The tangle and the bump threw Jennie onto her butt and pulled the bike down onto her lap.

She sat there under the machine for just a moment however. She was on her feet as though preparing for a bow by the time the doctor's whole self emerged from the back of the wagon and pulled the horse to a halt.

So this is the witch of Potawatomie, Doctor Fiddledog said to himself. *How fortunate.* Then he hopped down from the carriage, still carrying his fiddle, saying, "Oh, my, my. Oh, my, my, my. Are you all right?"

Miss Jennie was brushing herself off by then. "I just got this bike *fixed*." She pulled her lower lip into her mouth and stared at the doctor hard enough to stare a hole right through him if that were possible. "What do you think you're doing, taking up both sides of the road, letting a horse do the driving—even if it is a horse that has a good deal more brains than the man that owns it?"

"Well, begging your pardon," said the doctor, "surely I am to blame." He wanted to add, "Imagine a man thinking a mere mile of open prairie on either side of the road would be berth enough for a spinster on a bicycle to avoid a head-on collision with a plodding, one-horse wagon. And on such a clear day." But he decided against it. What he did add was, "I do hope your two-wheeler has not unduly suffered."

Jennie pulled the bike up on its tires and rocked it back and forth to see that was still in working order. Meanwhile the rustling and barking coming from the basket tied to the back of the bike drew the doctor's attention away from the pleasantries with the old woman.

"Don't you think you should check on your dog?" he said, pointing with the bow of his fiddle at the basket that was still secure on the back of Miss Jennie's bike.

"And get myself bit again by the horrid beast? It was all I could do to get it in the basket. I do not think so. I've incurred injuries enough from the reckless piloting of that caravan of yours. There are laws, you know, against driving without a driver. Laws that you can be sure Sheriff Hafstripe will be more than happy to enforce the moment I call his attention to them. So I suggest you get yourself up on that seat and direct that nag to hightail it out of Pottawatomie County with all the haste its creaking joints can muster if you don't want to spend the night in the Pottawatomie County jail."

To this the doctor was inclined to say, "If you think my four-year-old gelding is a nag, then you do not have the ocular capacity to operate a two-wheeled vehicle on a public road—which, if I may be so bold, explains perfectly how you could fail to get out of the way of a twelve-foot wagon with two miles of open road to do it in."

But he didn't say it. He knew of more useful ways to talk to the Jennie Griersons of the world. Besides, something very odd happened before he had the chance to say anything at all.

A heavy strand of rope brushed the back of his head, knocking his hat off. It crossed the space between him and Miss Jennie in a slow, meandering way, bobbing a little up and down. It appeared to be a heavy hemp cord made for tying down strong loads. But how was it that a piece of rope was dangling from the sky? And what passing cloud could it possibly be attached to?

He and Jennie looked ever so quickly at each other's blank faces and then, together, lifted their gazes along the path of the rope.

About twenty feet above them, slowly descending, was the perfect square bottom of a large wicker basket, black against the circumference of the colorful circle of a balloon that floated above it. Their mouths fell open so wide that if there had been someone in the basket with a pitcher of water, he probably could have poured the contents into their stomachs without its ever touching their teeth, or even their tongues.

The doctor suddenly felt as though he had always wanted a hot air balloon. People would come from miles around to take a ride in such a contraption and would pay a pretty penny to do it. Securing his fiddle under his arm, he grabbed the rope.

The rope went limp in his hand. The balloon was inching down. But then it started to rise, and it occurred to him that if it indeed took off, he would lose it, or, worse, it would lift him off the ground and he'd find himself dangling and kicking at the end of it like a small dog that wouldn't let go of a toy—and that would not be good for business. So, for help, he quickly tied the end of it around the nearest object: the handlebars of Miss Jennie's bike.

Miss Jennie opened her mouth to protest, but before she could get a word out, he said, "Just until I can get enough slack to tie it to the wagon."

But the balloon bobbed too far from the wagon to supply the doctor with any slack at all.

"Help me get it down," he said rather hotly to the dumbstruck woman.

Jennie didn't help him get it down. She went to free her bike.

But then again, she thought, what if this balloon did fly away with her bike—with that nuisance of a dog still strapped to the back of it? Well wouldn't that solve her problem in the simplest of manners? But then, she would have to buy another bike.

She paused to think about it.

"Grab the rope," the doctor yelled, "and pull for all you're worth."

In her own mind, Miss Jennie Grierson was worth quite a lot. But if you were to ask Jennie's banker or anyone else in Wamego, Jennie's worth did not amount to very much. So how much force did the doctor expect there to be in her pulling?

This was not a question that occurred to anyone.

Nor need it have. Jennie Grierson did not take orders, not from anyone, not even from the sheriff. She certainly did not take them from a run-down carnival showman. She refused to pull on the rope.

The balloon bobbed lower. It fell almost to the ground. Dr. Fiddledog dropped his fiddle and bow into the basket to get a better purchase on the side.

And that's when the sacks of ballast caught Miss Jennie's eye. Printed across them, in plain, bold, black letters, was one word: "EMERALDS."

"Emeralds?" she said.

You could do a lot of things with a whole sack of emeralds.

Of course no one in the world could believe that a balloon would use sacks of actual emeralds for ballast. As everyone knows, balloons use bags of sand. But one of these bags had a small tear in it, and through the tear Jennie could clearly see that the contents of the bag were of a dark green color. Emerald green. And more than that, as she was staring at the green through the hole in the bag, one small stone trickled out. With the quick athleticism of her dancing days, she reached out and caught it as it fell.

There, in the palm of her hand, lay a cut gemstone, dark, and yet seeming almost translucent. She did not have time to wonder if it was real, for the balloon just then started to rise once again. The doctor pulled himself up until he was hanging over the edge, half in and half out, and Jennie did exactly the same thing on the other side of the basket.

At just that moment a breeze kicked up. The balloon rose. Across the top of the basket the doctor's head was so close to Jennie's that they could have kissed—though it didn't occur to either one to do that—and their feet were dangling hazardously over the quickly receding ground. The weight of the bike at the end of the rope did not help in the least to slow the upward force on the balloon. The bike fluttered like the tail of a kite as the balloon raced for the clouds.

Jennie was the first to hoist herself up and into the basket. And, as proof that she had qualities other than meanness, she grabbed hold of the doctor and hauled him to safety as well. It did not occur to her to pull up the bike.

4

Meanwhile in the Emerald City of Oz, the Scarecrow, the Tin Man, and the Cowardly Lion were hunched over a big, green machine that was covered in lights and buttons. Many of the buttons had letters under them, such as "LT, RT, UP, DN," and some also had arrows beside them, N↗, S↖, E↙, W↘, and some just had arrows: ↑, ↓, ↖, ↘.

It was very confusing.

There was also a screen that was a little like a magic picture. It was green, and on it a yellow line moved in different ways and got brighter or dimmer when the switches clicked and a little stationary ball was rolled or certain levers were raised and lowered in a certain sequence.

Not even the Scarecrow, with his superior brain, could make heads nor tails of the contraption at first, although he played with it night and day for many days in a row. Having neither need to eat nor sleep, and having a newly minted curiosity as well as infinite patience, there was really no end to how long he could take to learn the secrets of this machine. Nor was there anything else interesting happening in the city to distract him.

With the Wizard gone, he was now the appointed ruler of the Emerald City, of course, but it didn't take a lot of effort to rule such a well-appointed city, one that had recently lost its only outside enemy and which did not do anything to make inside enemies. At the end of three or four days, he supposed he'd figured out the purpose of several buttons. And he called the Tin Man and the Cowardly Lion over to see what he had done.

"See here," he said. "This button controls the light in an up-down motion. And this one in a left-right motion. And this one makes it go in a diagonal this way, and these move it diagonally in the other directions." He flicked buttons and pointed at the moving light on the screen as he spoke. Of course he wasn't just flicking the switches. He was also moving the levers and rolling the stationary ball and turning a wheel, all of which made the light go fast or slow or made it grow bright and large or dim and small, like a candle flame getting closer or going farther away.

The Tin Man thought the Scarecrow was brilliant to have learned to control the light so well, and he patted his old friend on the back. The Lion thought the Scarecrow was very brave to play with a complicated machine such as this without knowing what it really did.

"What do you mean?" the Scarecrow asked. "It moves the light on this screen."

"Who knows?" he said. "Perhaps when you hit those switches you are using the machine to make a lovely lady dance or a terrible beast jump up and down or a ball of fire grow large or small somewhere."

The Scarecrow hadn't thought of that. He had focused all his attention on the light on the screen. But perhaps the light was a kind of picture of something in the real world. He stopped pressing buttons and flicking switches so that he could give the matter a little thought.

5

The balloon dipped and jumped and jittered as it raced through the sky. The doctor hunched in the bottom of the basket clutching his violin while Jennie leaned over the edge and watched the ground flying by. She wondered at moments of dip if she might be able to swing the bike at the end of the rope like a ship's anchor into the top of a tree. When the balloon got really low, she even thought of sliding down the rope to get closer to the ground. But the opportunity to do that quickly passed and they were on their way back to the clouds.

Sometimes they came so close to the ground that the bike at the end of the rope nearly touched the tops of the grass. But every time they dipped almost close enough to the earth to make Jennie think it might be safe to jump, they rose again as quickly as they fell, and they were always just a bit too high to risk it. Sometimes the balloon ascended high above the clouds, where it was so cold that the passengers huddled together in the bottom of the basket under the doctor's jacket—something that no force on the ground in Kansas ever would have led them to do. Land and trees and mountains and even an ocean sped by underneath them. Sometimes they looked down on birds and, once, even on an airplane. Sometimes the bike brushed the waves of the ocean so that spray came up in their faces (by that point, the doctor had worked up the courage to stand up and look down).

What made them think (although neither said it aloud) that the balloon was indeed *taking* them somewhere was the speed at which it traveled. Although it bobbed up and down like a rubber ball in the hands of a child, and although it went sometimes fast and sometimes faster, its swift course through the sky never seemed to match the speed and direction of the wind. Something seemed to be pulling them.

Both the doctor and Miss Jennie were standing and leaning over the edge of the basket when the balloon finally came down in a steadily slowing way that made them hope it was finally thinking about landing.

From over the transom, they saw deep woods and then a dark castle on the top of a mountain. The castle was surrounded by many jagged peaks. Its many large turrets and maze-like walls gave it an ominous look, and the shadows of the mountains that lay across it made it appear damp and foreboding. Still, Jennie and the doctor hoped the balloon was heading for the wide-open courtyard and not for the jagged cliffs.

There was a tree on the inner side of the paved courtyard. It was black and leafless and had the jagged form of a fruit tree in winter. And yet it was much larger than any fruit tree either Jennie or the doctor had ever seen. The balloon bobbed down toward it as though it had been the goal of the whole flight. And when it got near, Jennie did manage to do what she had wanted to do all the way back in Kansas. She swung the bike at the end of its rope until it caught in the branches and held fast, shaking the tree all over. From there she and the doctor were able to pull on the rope to lower the balloon until they could grab onto the branches of the tree and climb out.

As soon as the doctor shifted his weight from the basket to the branch, he let go of the balloon, expecting it to rise, perhaps even to pull free of the branch. And this was something he hoped to avoid because he knew—although he had not brought it up during the flight—that there was a dog in the basket on the back of the bike.

The truth is that Doctor Fiddledog and Miss Jennie had not exchanged a single word during the entire time they were in the air.

But the balloon did not pull against the branch. Relieved of his weight, the balloon rose and fell gently and seemed to wiggle in the air—although at the same time it appeared that the tree was shaking itself free of the balloon. But whether the air was pulling on the balloon or the branches were quivering to get clear of it, the movement went on until the bike was freed from the branch.

And then it went down, down toward the ornate floor. Clear of the tree, the balloon seemed to lay the bike down as gently as a leaf lands that a tree has dropped. The balloon too fluttered down until it seemed to settle itself on the courtyard floor. It was sitting placidly down before either the doctor or Jennie managed to disentangle themselves from the high branches of the tree. It almost seemed to be waiting for them to climb down.

The first thing Doctor Fiddledog did once he was out of the entanglement of the tree was to kneel down by the basket that was strapped to the back of the bike. He had heard barking sounds now and then during the flight. But it had been several hours since he had heard anything, and he was worried that whatever was in the basket was no longer alive.

The basket was padlocked—a measure he thought more than could possibly be needed to keep a dog inside. He did not ask Jennie for the key. He pulled his pen knife from his pocket and cut the leather strap away from the wicker top.

In the bottom of the basket was a black lump. It wasn't moving. He reached his hands into the basket expecting the worst. But the fur was warm. As soon as he touched it, the sleeping dog opened its eyes and yapped and leaped from the basket, stretching its legs the moment it hit the ground. Then it came right up to Morgan and licked his hand. Around its neck was a collar and a tag. And on the tag was the word "Toto."

"Hello, Toto," the doctor said. And Toto wagged his tail and raised himself up and licked Morgan's face and made him laugh. "What a wonderful little dog."

Toto ran a quick lap around the courtyard, barked once and then twice at Miss Jennie, and then put his paws on Doctor Morgan's shin, asking to be picked up. "You have a wonderful dog, Miss Jennie."

Miss Jennie huffed and groaned and said nothing.

"I've always believed that a dog reflects the character of its owner. And if this playful and friendly little dog is yours, there must be more to you than I have heard."

"It's not mine," she said over her shoulder.

While the doctor was rescuing Toto, Miss Jennie was attempting to secure the balloon. They had come a long, long way in this vehicle. And she had hated every moment of the voyage. The sight of the balloon was less welcome to her eyes than sight of the cyclone had been, and the feel of the ground beneath her feet was as wonderful as she imagined the feel of the stage of the New York Ballet would have been if she had ever made it there. But this balloon was the thing that had gotten them to wherever they were, and she knew it may well be that they would need it again if they were ever to get back home. And even in her moment of greatest dread, she could not be sure that she might not be persuaded to climb back into this death trap. She needed at least to keep the option open. So she leaned into the basket and pulled a second rope out and ran it to the tree and tied it around the trunk with a knot strong enough to hold an angry bull.

"There," she said, exhaling.

But then the tree began to rustle. The sound reminded both her and the doctor of a grumbling yawn. Toto ran to the tree and sniffed it. He lifted his leg and peed on the rope. The trembling in the tree became an all-over shaking; its leafless branches and its wide, solid trunk shimmied like a dancer that had no rhythm and then like a palsied old man. It wiggled and shook until the rope vibrated up its trunk. It was perhaps the most amazing thing either Miss Jennie or the doctor had ever seen. As the rope inched upward, the tree made noises like those of a sick man clearing his throat to speak after a long nap. Up the trunk the rope inched. When it got to the lowest branches, the branches folded in like arms. The doctor's mouth fell open. Jennie's eyes grew to twice their normal size. Little twigs on the branches wrapped around the thick knot Jennie had tied, and pulled at it. Jennie ran up to the tree to grab the rope, but the branch reached out to her and slapped her hand away.

She slapped back. And she was slapped back again. She went for the rope, but the strong branch with finger-like twigs wrapped itself around her wrist and held her still while other branches and twigs worked out the knot.

"Stop this infernal tree," she yelled to the doctor. But he did not move. "That's our ride home," she yelled, pulling with her free hand at the twigs that held her. The doctor did not charge the tree. He grabbed the bike. He sat on the seat just as the tree freed the rope from its waist and flung it aside. The tree flung Jennie aside at the same time so that she fell on her hands and knees.

The balloon rose.

The doctor rose with it.

Jennie jumped to her feet and *jetéd* from the tree to the bike. But she did not grab hold. The doctor hovered at about the height her head.

"What do you think you are doing?" she said.

"Endeavoring to hold down the balloon so it can't get away."

"It carried you over an ocean. What makes you think you are man enough to hold it down?"

"I may not have thought this through," he said. And then he let go of the bike. There was nothing they could do.

Jennie felt a twinge and reached for her knee.

6

The Scarecrow had thought everything thoroughly through. He was now certain that there was something in the real world that he was controlling with the knobs, the wheels, the levers, and the switches.

And that thing was the Wizard's balloon.

"How did you figure *that* out?" the Tin Man wanted to know.

"And what makes you think you *have* figured it out?" the Lion wondered aloud.

"My brilliant brains," said the Scarecrow. "Do you remember the last thing the Wizard said before he left us that fateful day?"

"Goodbye?"

"No," said the Scarecrow.

"Oh, yes, I think that *was* it," the Cowardly Lion said. "I remember him waving at everyone as he said it."

"No, no, I mean before that."

"I hope I don't crash in the deadly desert?" the Tin Man said.

"No, no, after that," said the Scarecrow.

"I hope I find my way back to the circus?" said the Lion.

"I'll just tell you," the Scarecrow said. "He said, 'How the heck does this thing work?'"

"He *did* say that," the Lion said.

"And that's exactly what *I* said the moment I saw this contraption. Remember? You, Tin Man, said 'Can you make it make the talking head of a lovely lady? I'd like to see that.' And you, Lion, said, 'Oh, please don't. That was scary.' And then you, Tin Man, said, 'Maybe we can make it into a smiling beast. Can you do it, Scarecrow?' And I said, '*How the heck does this thing work?*'" And the Scarecrow attempted a facial expression that would have meant, "See, isn't it obvious now what we've thought about it?" if a burlap sack were capable of that much expression.

The Scarecrow pressed some buttons and turned some wheels.

"What are you doing now?" said the Tin Man.

"I'm bringing the balloon back to the Emerald City. With any luck, the Wizard will still be in it."

"Then you won't have to be the ruler of the Emerald City anymore," said the king of beasts.

"Yes, I'm tired of ruling anyway. Well, not *tired* exactly. I don't get tired. But I'd rather be exploring the great and wonderful Land of Oz than sitting on a throne in a richly appointed city and staring at green rocks all day. I know that as a king yourself you may not understand that some of us were not born to rule."

"Some of us were not born at all," said the Tin Man.

The Scarecrow's hopes were dashed when the balloon landed without the wizard inside. Everyone rejoiced in the whole city to see the great foreign contrivance sway down from the sky. A large crowd of citizens in wide-brimmed green hats swarmed to the street where the Wizard's familiar balloon rocked itself down. But then the first citizen to climb the steps beside the spot where the Scarecrow had gently and expertly landed it peered over the edge and down into the bottom of the basket and pronounced it empty.

But it had not come back without anything. There was something with two wheels and what looked like handles and a seat that came dangling down beneath it.

"What is that?" the assembled crowd cried.

"I don't know," the Scarecrow said.

"Is it alive?" a citizen wanted to know.

"It doesn't have a heartbeat," said the Tin Man.

"That won't do," said the Lion, who, despite his courage, was a little scared of it. "A leader needs to present definite answers for all questions."

"Even if he doesn't have them?" said the Scarecrow.

"Especially if he doesn't have them," said the Lion. "That's what makes the job so scary."

"I know what it is," said the Tin Man, who was standing beside the Scarecrow and holding onto the thing by its apparent handles. "It's a clue."

After a good deal of back and forth between the three, they declared that a clue was exactly what it was—a clue about the fate of the wizard. And it was decided that the three of them would set about to study the clue further.

"If we can figure out what it's for and how it works, we may be able to figure out more."

"What more?" said the Lion.

"I don't know yet. Perhaps we'll need to figure out what the rest of it looks like."

"The rest of it?" said the Tin Man.

"Of course," said the Scarecrow. "There are certainly missing pieces. Here we have handles, and here we have a seat, and here we have wheels. But if you sit on the seat and hold the handles, you tumble." He demonstrated to prove his point. "So there must be missing pieces that hold it up and also pieces that make it, well, do whatever it does."

And the Lion and the Tin Man noted again the brilliant thinking of the Scarecrow's excellent brains.

7

The bulging eyes of the thick-trunked, gnarly-branched tree snapped open.

Jennie and the doctor jumped back, and almost grabbed one another.

It was one thing to see a tree untie a knot with its finger-like branches. It was another to see it sneer at you with shadowy looks.

As soon as they saw the eyes, they saw something more. The tree had a face. Under its eyes was a fat, stubby branch that was clearly a nose, and under the nose a horizontal slit that was clearly a mouth.

"We are a long way from Kansas," the doctor said.

The tree moved four arm-like limbs toward them, and then pushed the limbs down in the direction of its feet, or rather its roots—at least, they hoped what it had was roots and not feet, because if it had feet it might come for them.

It spoke one parched word: "water."

The doctor advanced slowly with his hands out in front of him to show the tree he meant it no harm. It did not move.

"I wouldn't go near it," Jennie said, learning forward.

The doctor moved closer. Toto stood beside Jennie and barked.

"Suit yourself," she said. "But if it tears you apart, it will not be any of my fault."

She stood up straight; Doctor Morgan kneeled when he got to the tile edge of the circle of dirt around the base of the tree. He felt the soil.

"Dry as a Kansas wind," he said. He dug into the soil as far as he easily could with his pocket knife. There was no sign of moisture. "This tree needs water."

He got up and he bowed before the tree. Toto ran a tight circle and barked.

"I don't know why you'd want to preserve the thing that robbed us of our only hope of ever getting home," Jennie said. "Besides, where could we even find water?"

"Well, maybe I'll just ask the tree?" he said. "Where can I find water?"

The tree shook all over but did not talk.

"It doesn't know," Jennie said.

So the doctor with Toto at his side explored the castle. He did not ask Jennie to help, but after a few minutes standing alone in the wide courtyard with an evil-looking tree staring at her, she decided to go as well. She did not help in the search for water, however. She wanted to find out whose castle she was intruding in, and whether they were friendly, and, if not, how much she'd have to pay to make them so. What a shame it was that she hadn't managed to get even one of those sacks of emeralds from the balloon.

No one seemed to be home. But the castle did seem to have been lived in pretty recently. There was unspoiled food in the galley, and there was a little water—very little water—in buckets here and there.

Toto, running around as directly as if he knew the place, led the doctor to some of these scattered buckets. These the doctor spilled on the ground at the tree's roots. But it was like watering a sunflower with a thimble. Eventually the little dog (he must have had a nose for water) led him to a small room far away that had a pump in it. The room had a heavy door that was difficult to open; it seemed as though whoever had built this place didn't want water too readily available. But why anyone would treat water that way, he could not imagine. Perhaps it was why no one lived here anymore.

Even with the larger bucket he found in the room, he had to countless trips from one end of the castle to the other to water to the tree while Jennie explored the castle.

At first the water sat on the dirt as though he had been poured on concrete. And then it slowly bubbled in. And then, as more buckets were poured, it disappeared under the dirt ever more quickly. At that point, the tree uttered sounds of relief, and then sounds of pleasure, and then finally it started to talk.

At first all it said was "more water, more water." And the doctor brought buckets until he thought he would collapse. "How much more?" he said. But the tree just said, "more water, more water." Well if a tree could talk, you wouldn't expect it to be brilliant, would you? He brought more water; he poured out buckets until the soil around the tree became muddy, until it could no longer absorb any more water. But the tree said again, "more water."

"You're full," said the doctor.

Jennie leaned against the rail of a high stone bridge and shouted down at the doctor to stop with the useless watering of a dying tree—she knew a dying tree when she saw one—and told him to focus his energy on their real problems: finding out where they were, who owned the castle, whether the people of this place were friendly or hostile, and whether there was any chance of getting their balloon back. They might also think of finding a way out of the castle and down the mountain. She'd found a gate and a drawbridge in her exploring, but no way to open the one or lower the other. Still, whoever lived here was bound to be back sooner or later, and it was not certain that they would be happy to find intruders.

The doctor looked up and said merely, "Have you not considered the possibility that a talking tree could give us the information you are looking for?"

Not that he himself thought it could, but the question did quiet Miss Jennie who could only respond, as though she hoped it was useful information, "It's a tree."

Eyes wide open and starting to tear up, the tree stared straight ahead and made a straining face—and a leaf popped out on the end of its nose.

"I'm full," the tree said. And its mouth smiled and it seemed delighted.

Then it reached down with long branches and finger-like twigs and hoisted the doctor off the ground by his shoulders and scowled.

Jennie put a hand to her mouth and ran toward the courtyard.

Toto exploded in barking and charged at the tree.

"Now what do you mean, tying a rope to my trunk? You trying to cut me down? You trying to carry me away?" The tree held the doctor tight by his two arms and shook him as though it were trying to get his leaves to fall.

Toto barked and ran around the trunk and clawed at the roots. He picked a spot and dug in with his little claws as though he were digging for a bone.

"What? *You* again? Hey, stop that," the tree yelled. "Stop him."
But Toto kept barking and digging.

The tree dropped the doctor and started shaking all over and
lowing its branches and swinging them back and forth to get at the
digging dog. But it could not reach him.

Jennie arrived, running and hopping and grabbing at her knee.
She was headed toward the tree. But the doctor held her back by
raising his hand. Toto kept digging.

"Stop that, I say. You'll unroot me. Stop him, stop him, stop him."

"Toto," the doctor yelled. "That's enough."

Toto turned and peed in the hole he'd dug and ran back to the doctor and Jennie.

8

The crabby tree was the only source of information the doctor and Jennie had about where they were, and information was indispensable if they were to find a way to get home. But the tree volunteered almost nothing and rarely bothered to speak when spoken to.

What to do?

The doctor sat a chair in front of it and pulled a bottle of Dr. Morgan's Magical Elixir from an inner pocket of his coat (there were precious few bottles left since he and Jennie had drunk most of the ones he'd had with him during their flight in the balloon). He downed the single dose, then he put his fiddle to his chin and began to play. Perhaps a tune would improve the tree's mood.

And perhaps it did, a little. The tree did not open its eyes. But it said nothing nasty or challenging while the music played. And its branches trembled ever so slightly the whole time. But if it was not unfriendly while the music played, it was its crabby old self again the moment the music stopped.

"Is that how you get trees to talk where you come from?"

"Trees don't talk where I come from."

"Not until you cut them down and hollow them out and torment them with branches," the tree quipped.

It took a moment for the doctor realize it was referring to the fiddle.

Although the tree never became friendly, its mood improved a little once its leaves began to sprout. It sprouted leaves and then blossoms and then, in little while, fruit. The speed of all this growth was astonishing. What would have taken weeks in Kansas happened in just days in this place, whatever this place was. It seemed to grow every kind of fruit that grows on trees: apples of many kinds, but also pears and cherries and oranges and grapefruit and plums and citrons and figs and lemons. But it wasn't the growth of fruit any more than music that got it to give useful answers to important questions. It was the threat of sending Toto to dig at its roots that did that, that is, as long as Toto was at the castle. And the threat of not watering it got the tree to talk after Toto left.

But they still couldn't be sure they could trust anything the tree said. The first thing it said, once it got a good look at Jennie, made no sense at all. It said, "I see you're back."

"You see my what?" Jennie said. She was facing the tree at the time.

"Oh," said the tree. "So that's the game." And then it brought a branch to the back of its head and scratched itself. "So do we have another plan to get the shoes?"

"I don't know who you think I am," said Jennie.

"Of course you don't. You can drain the chlorophyll and change the face but you will still look the same to a tree."

"I have no idea what you're talking about. I doubt you can see half as well as you pretend to."

"Hmmm," the tree said. "Perhaps you're not you after all. Then you must be one of your long-lost sisters, or why else would you have come here?"

"I did not 'come' here. I was dragged here by a balloon. You were there."

"Was I? Memory's a little wintery. I was half asleep and almost dead at the time."

"We need your help," the doctor said.

"Do you? And yet I'm bored with you already," the tree said. "But as long as you water me, I don't really care where you get your powers. What do you want?"

It told them that the name of the land they were in was Oz, and that the Land of Oz, having lost its wizard, was ruled by a scarecrow. (The Kansas folk did not know what to make of that.) It said this castle belonged to "your sister, of course," that it had long been protected by magic, by "Winkie guards," whom the tree also called "slaves," as well as by monkeys with wings. The tree said no one lived there anymore and that it itself had gone unwatered for quite some time, weeks, or maybe months. It never rained there. It told them that it could communicate, by means of its roots, to any tree in Oz, although it couldn't be quite sure they'd talk back. But that still made it a good sentry, which is why the witch had brought it there. And it offered them the same deal it had offered "your sister": as long as they would water it, it would give them news of anything in the whole land that might be of use to them, and it would not try to tear the two of them apart. The doctor agreed, but Jennie told it directly that it was a dangerous thing to have around, that it was full of untrustworthy information and that if it did have anything useful to say, it had probably already said it, and that as soon as she found an ax, she would turn it into firewood, fruit or no fruit, if it gave her any occasion to do so.

"Then who will protect you from your enemies?" The tree did not seem concerned by her threat.

"I have no enemies," she said.

At this the tree laughed.

"That's what you think," said the tree. "My roots run deep. I may not tell you everything I know, but if any of these enemies you do not have approach your castle, I will give you warning. Whatever you think of me, you can be sure I will protect any reliable source of water. That should be security enough to maintain me for a while, don't you think? In fact," it went on before they could respond, "to prove my worth, your Winkies are on their way as we speak. They'll be here by morning."

Toto was already long gone by then. The doctor had looked for him everywhere, called his name and listened for his bark. But there was no sign of him. Doctor Fiddledog thought this might serve as the first test of the tree's abilities.

"What has happened to Toto?"

The tree frowned and shifted its mouth back and forth. "Oh," it said, "has my enemy scattered? Well, good riddance."

"But where is he?"

"Oh, you really want to know. Well, hmmm. A little beast in a great land, that may take some time to discover. I'll ask around."

Meanwhile the doctor also wanted to know why these Winkies were coming to see them.

"They think the witch has returned."

"And when they find that Jennie is not the witch, I suppose they will leave."

"Well she may not be *the* witch but you won't convince me or them that she is not *a* witch. And if there is a witch in this castle overlooking the land of the Winkies, they will certainly come."

"How did they even know she was here?"

"They were called by the fires she has been burning in the evenings."

"But we were just cooking," said the doctor.

He and Jennie had found a small greenhouse on the southern side of the castle. It was watered by the pump in the pump room, which somehow pumped whether there was anyone there to pump the handle or not, so the vegetables had remained watered, ripe and healthy while the tree had nearly withered away. There was also oil and flour in the kitchen, and there were chickens in a coop just off the side of the greenhouse. It was a marvelous find. Jennie wrung the neck of a chicken while the doctor pulled potatoes and carrots and plucked tomatoes and eggplants, and they put them together in the large kitchen in the basement of the castle and had a feast.

The doctor said he would gladly do all the cooking if Jennie would do all the wringing of chickens' necks, as neck wringing was not a thing he enjoyed, whereas to her it was as easy as swatting a fly or kicking a dog.

"Where do you suppose Toto has got to?" the doctor asked soon after he'd decided the dog was missing and before he'd asked the tree.

"Can't be far enough away for me," Jennie said. "Been afraid for my ankles every moment since you hauled it out of that basket." She was opening cabinets in search of a broom. Instead she found two black hats. They were long and pointed, and apparently never used. And they fit perfectly.

The doctor squared up a head of lettuce for his cleaver. "That's a

very pretty hat," he said. "I hope you're hungry."

"I'm sure the owner would not mind," she said, laying a hand on the brim. "But why would you cook for me?"

"You mean because you don't like me?"

"I can't abide a squeamish man," she said.

"Or anyone who lives in Potawatomie Country in any way you disapprove of?"

"You don't *live* there. You don't pay taxes. You don't support the schools or the government. You're a mountebank and a bum. You make money by taking money from the foolish and gullible. So, no, I don't like you. And what's more, I don't approve of you."

"I wouldn't think you'd mind what happens to the money of the foolish and gullible."

"No, I don't care much what happens to their pennies. If they want to throw them away on the disappointing hopes of a confidence man, that's nothing to me," she said. "But you give the county a bad reputation. And that is something I cannot abide. And if we can't get rid of you and your kind, which seem to be growing like a fungus throughout the county, we will be overrun by lazy, homeless, lack-laws. And I will not abide that. Honest people get their money by the sweat of their brow not the oiling of their tongues."

He wanted to say, "Don't you mean by the sweat of their father's brows and by the sweat of their father's laborers," but he didn't think that would move the conversation along the proper path.

He was chopping onions at the time; Jennie was pacing the floor, now and then throwing fuel on the fire to keep the room and the oven hot.

"You're also a bad influence on the morals of the youth of the county," she said.

"Like Claire," he said through tears.

Jennie stopped pacing.

"How do you know about Claire?"

"People talk," he said. "When I sell them false dreams at my little wagon, people talk to me. And you may want to know: they talk a lot about you."

"No, I do not want not know that, and I certainly do not want to know what they say." Jennie threw a shovel of coal into the firebox of the huge cast iron stove.

"Is she as big a disappointment to you as I am?" the doctor asked, "Claire, I mean."

"Ha. Far bigger," she said. "You're not a disappointment, as I never had any expectations for you. You, you're a nuisance, like that talking tree. Claire heard ridiculous stories from ages ago and decided she wanted to be an artist. Thought I would approve."

The doctor managed to bring his tears under control and to set to work on the rutabagas and carrots.

"How odd," he said. "I guess she heard that you once wanted to be a dancer."

"Well, it does not surprise me that the sort of people who talk to you are the sort of people who tell other people what is none of their business. But yes, that's true. I wish I could deny it. I was as foolish as my niece when I was young. When I was a girl, I had a girl's dreams. And I was very lucky to be rescued from them before they destroyed me, as they will destroy Claire, if no one can stop her."

Jennie finally managed to locate a broom and began to sweep the floor.

"I see," said the doctor, although he didn't think he saw what he thought Jennie wanted him to see.

"She's the closest relative I have," she said. "I have raised her to take over the house and the farm and the family name when her turn comes. It is a big responsibility."

"I see," the doctor said again. There were a lot of other things he wanted to say, but these seemed to be the words that oiled the machinery of Jennie's tongue when it was about to grind to a halt, so he stuck with them.

"I don't think you do. And I don't know why I'm telling you. But I'll tell you this, that girl had the gumption to come to me and beg me to pay her way to New York, to set her up at an arts academy they have there and even to help her get into art shows. Art shows," she stuck out her tongue, "nothing more than the polished and spit-shined cousin of the pathetic little con business you yourself are in. Don't think I'm fooled. Supply it with the wherewithal deck itself in fancy marquees and satin dresses and it may look as pretty as a chocolate cake with marshmallows and strawberries, but at its heart it's no different from a mountebank in a stolen circus wagon selling panaceas of vodka and peppermint oil."

"You do put a period on it, I'll give you that," said the doctor.

"If you try to sell me a piece of painted cardboard and call it chocolate cake, I for one will know the difference."

"So you told her you wouldn't help her?" The doctor was sniffing at the holes on the tops of various shakers of what seemed to be spices to see if he could find something he recognized.

"Utterly refused," said Jennie. "Forbade it in fact. She tried to go anyway, without any money. I threatened to disinherit her. Even that didn't stop her."

"And did you disinherit her?" he asked.

"I am a woman of my word."

"I see," he said, although he was not sure what she'd said was precisely as clear as a "yes" or a "no."

"Anyway, that's none of your business," she said.

"I merely thought if we were stuck here together, we might want to talk, you know. To pass the time."

"Are you ready to put the chicken in the oven?"

Although they could not see it from the basement kitchen, the smoke that billowed from the chimney was a brilliant cloud of pink.

9

Toto found a hole in the base of an outer wall of the castle. It was just big enough for a little dog to squeeze through. Outside, he sniffed the air and picked up, faintly, out of the haze of dirt and rot and smoke, a clean and trailing scent of bricks and flowers. It came from the direction of the sunrise. He wound his way down the familiar mountain and smelled a path to the Emerald City. If there were evil creatures lurking in the dark forest, he didn't see any, and they left him alone.

When he got to the Emerald City, the people there left him alone as well. He walked right through the open door and scurried directly across the grounds to the door where not a very long time before Dorothy had taken him to meet the wizard. He passed countless people in green garments, laughing and chattering and even singing. No one gave him a second look.

The door that led to the throne room was not open or closed. It was gone altogether. Apparently, the new ruler or rulers of the city didn't see any reason to stop any citizen of Oz from coming to see them at any time for any reason without an appointment.

Toto marched fearlessly into the wide chamber, and he ran directly to the spot where there used to be a curtain. There was no one there.

He barked once.

The Scarecrow, the Tin Man, and the Lion came running from the throne where they had been trying to figure out the two-wheeled contraption that had come down with the wizard's balloon. It was sitting on the throne. They were still trying to work out what the pieces they needed to make it work might look like.

"Dorothy's back?" said the Lion, scooping Toto fearlessly into his arms.

Toto licked his face.

"I wonder," said the Scarecrow.

"And Toto wants to lead us to her," said the Tin Man.

"And then maybe she can tell us how that machine works," said the Lion, glancing at it.

10

The Winkie guards showed up in their full uniforms and carrying their halberds. Then came the monkeys with wings.

Jennie and the doctor were not taken by surprise. Although the crabby tree (which by then had produced bushels of the finest tasting fruit anyone had ever tasted) had had no luck in finding Toto, it had told them about the monkeys with wings many hours before they landed.

Perhaps they could trust the tree after all.

It had to clarify again that its knowledge was limited to Oz (the doctor had hoped it might be able to stretch its influence clear to Kansas so that he could find out what had become of his horse and wagon). But within Oz, it knew a lot of things, even if it couldn't easily locate one little dog.

Doctor Fiddledog found that if he just kept the tree watered, it had a lot to say. It told him marvelous things about the Land of Oz—and not just because it had to. It might be crabby, but it was also lonely, and it liked to talk. The doctor learned about a green city and a long road of yellow brick. He learned about a colorful land of little people who lived close together in mushroom-shaped houses where there was a statue of a girl and of a dog that looked like the dog he was looking for. (This was so far the only little dog any Oz tree had been able to find.) The girl had a basket on her arm, and in the basket was a pair of sparkling shoes. It told him too of a bubble so large it could fit a whole person inside it, and inside the bubble was a whole person, a woman in a fancy white gown and a tall, pointed hat that looked like the black one Jennie never took off these days. The soap bubble was floating high in the sky, and the woman was smiling with a blissful expression. She seemed to be headed toward the green city. "There must be a story there," the doctor muttered to himself.

The tree also told him that Jennie, on the floor below him, in the basement kitchen, was sitting at the table, her head bowed, her shoulders quivering as though she were sobbing.

"How can you know that?" the doctor asked. "There are no trees in the kitchen."

"I have deep roots."

But why would Jennie be sobbing?

The doctor went downstairs. And he made a lot of noise and cleared his throat as he descended the stairs. "Miss Grierson," he said as he approached the doorway, "I think we have company."

When he crossed the threshold, she was sweeping the floor.

They went up to the top of a high tower and watched as a large troop of dark-faced soldiers with tall hats and uniforms in yellow and grey, and big yellow shoes that looked a lot like clown shoes marching in dictatorial formation to the front gate. One of them said something, and the gate rose and the drawbridge came down. And then they marched in columns into the castle.

When they saw the two Kansas folk, one of them snapped his feet together and called up.

"We came as soon as we heard you had returned."

"What do you suppose that means?" the doctor said.

Jennie did not pause to discuss the matter. She hurried down the stairs to confront the invading army.

"Remember, they are your slaves," said the tree before the Winkies had crossed the bridge into the courtyard.

Several dozen filled the courtyard and stood in strict military columns as though preparing for inspection.

Miss Jennie had no interest in inspecting troops, however. She was a little put off that she nonetheless felt an impulse to stand at attention and say, "Why have you come?" She fought the impulse, crossed her arms and said, "What do you want?"

The one who must have been the leader stared at her.

"Is your skin really that color?" she said.

"Your skin is not green," said the captain (she decided he was a captain).

"I should hope not."

"But the resemblance is close enough," he went on. "So it's true what we've heard. You are her sister."

So she knew he'd heard whatever he'd heard from the tree. Or at least it had started with the tree. If there really were talking trees all over this land, one of them had talked to this captain. She said, "I'm not anyone's sister."

"That's true," said the captain. "Both of your sisters are gone. We regret…"

She waved off the rest of the sentence. "What are you here for?"

That's when the doctor huffed down to her side, causing a loud but unintelligible whisper to run like a wave through the ranks of Winkies.

"So it's true you have captured the wizard. We will hold him here with you. His power is great. He may be a danger to Oz."

With a gesture, the captain ordered the portcullis lowered and the drawbridge raised.

"The wizard?" Jennie said.

But the doctor held up his hand in a gesture that asked her not to continue. To his surprise, she did not.

Doctor Morgan Fiddledog did not in fact look anything like the Great and Terrible Wizard of Oz. But the tree had told him that very few in all of Oz had ever seen the wizard. And if the Winkies wanted to believe he was this wizard, he saw no reason to correct them.

And then a shadow passed over their heads and a chattering sound, and a whole cloud the flying monkeys lighted in the courtyard like a flock of pigeons. The one in front wore a golden cap. Their formation was less orderly than that of the Winkie guards. In fact it was more of a puddle of primates than a formation. They jumped up and down and screeched like chimps. Jennie had to call on all the strength she had not to jump back cringing. The guards with halberds did not frighten her one bit. But large animals with sharp teeth put her on edge.

"I don't suppose we can talk to them," said the doctor.

"You can talk to them all you like," said Jennie. "The problem is having them talk to you. They're monkeys."

Over the heads of the monkeys they noticed the cranky fruit tree awkwardly waving them over with his big arm-like branches.

"Didn't your sister tell you ambuloids anything?" he said. "Those are your minions. If you want them to minion, give them orders.

Tell them what do to. These are the creatures that watered me when your sister was here. I sent word that you, pinch face, had come to take over your sister's reign and that you'd captured the wizard. The monkeys will live here again and will do whatever you ask them to do to."

"Why will they do that?" Jennie wanted to know.

"It's best not to ask," the tree said. "As for the Winkies, treat them like slaves. They hate you, but they're scared to death of you. You may not have all your sister's magic, but you'd better convince them you have some of her power if you don't want a bucket of water tossed at you."

Jennie looked over to the Winkies and put her fingers on her chin and squinted.

11

The four fearless adventurers—the Scarecrow, the Tin Man, the Lion, and Toto—paused just outside the wall of the Emerald City, waiting for the bubble to land.

They had not seen Glinda since the day Dorothy left Oz, and they were anxious to tell her of the girl's return. Instead Glinda told them of the news she had heard from a Winkie maiden who had overheard a tree telling it to a winged monkey: a new witch was in the castle, an unknown sister of the Witches of the East and West. She had captured the Wizard and Toto from the land of Kansas and brought them back to Oz. This new witch was holding the Wizard prisoner, making him cook and carry water for her.

"And is Dorothy a prisoner too?" the Lion said.

"It's possible," said Glinda, "although I have not heard anything of her. And yet, Toto would never leave Kansas without Dorothy if he could help it. Dorothy must be hidden deep in the castle."

"That makes sense," the Scarecrow said.

"But it's sad," said the Tin Man.

"This new sister hasn't flown anywhere since she arrived," Glinda said.

"So maybe she'll stay in the castle. So we'll have nothing to be afraid of," said the Lion.

"I believe that this," Glinda pointed to the bike, "this is her broomstick."

"And we almost took it right to her," said the Tin Man.

"Oh, but you must," said Glinda.

"Must we?" said the Tin Man.

Toto barked.

"Yes, I see that we must," the Scarecrow said. "We need to offer it to her in trade for Dorothy and the Wizard."

"But then she'll have a broomstick." The Tin Man quaked.

"A witch can always make another broomstick," Glinda said.

"Or we could just throw a bucket of water on her," the Lion said.

"That was an accident," said the Tin Man.

"We can accidentally throw a bucket of water on her," the Lion said.

"No," said the Scarecrow, adjusting his cap, "I do not think that would be honest."

"Dissolution may be more than she deserves," said Glinda.

"But she's enslaving the Wizard," said the Lion, "and holding Dorothy in her dungeon."

"Perhaps she is," said Glinda. "But all we really know is that the Wizard is there in the castle with her, cooking and hauling water. Hauling water to an evil tree isn't necessarily slavery."

"It may be an act of kindness," said the Tin Man.

"Maybe I'll just stay here," said the Lion.

"No, no, no," said the Scarecrow. "This will be a difficult adventure. We will need brains and heart and strength to see it through."

"And also a dog," said the Tin Man.

So with the Scarecrow holding one handle and the Tin Man holding the other handle and with Toto in the basket of the mechanized broomstick, the three courageous adventurers and the Lion headed toward the witch's castle.

12

The doctor wondered if the monkeys were strong enough to fly them all the way to Kansas. Jennie laughed. The gaggle of winged monkeys that were congregating in a corner of the room echoed her laughter in sounds that seemed almost scoffing. Jennie turned at them in disgust. She didn't like them. She especially didn't like that one with the golden cap that the rest seemed to follow. She would have run over and waved her arms to get rid of them like a flock of birds if she were not afraid they would bite her.

"No, I suppose not," the doctor said.

"The balloon ride was horrible enough," she said. "But how long will we be trapped in this musty fortress? Or shall we wander out in that wilderness—which I suppose is what we'll end up doing, though I doubt it will be any better."

"There must be some way to get where someone could help us. The tree says we'll never find any place better than this castle in all of Oz."

"But that's just what the tree would say because it needs us here to water it," Jennie said. "I don't trust it. And I don't trust those 'Winkies,' or I'd ask them."

"Or the monkeys."

"I wouldn't go to a barn if I knew those things were in it." Jennie stopped pacing the room. She sat on a cushion and rubbed her knee. Beside her was an ornate hourglass. She leaned over to get a closer look.

"I agree that the tree tells us what it wants us to know, but do you really think the Winkies cannot be trusted?"

"I don't trust anyone."

"I know you don't. But this time you may be right. Why can't people be more trusting? If only I had some of my cards or if we hadn't drunk all my elixir, I might be able to trade for good information."

"You mean if you hadn't tossed the empty bottles, you could have filled them with water and some of those odd spices from the kitchen and called yourself Houdini. How do you live with yourself?" Jennie picked up the hour glass and looked closely at the figures on its columns, "conning people out of their money with your bootleg and your tricks? Oh, if only I'd managed to get one of those bags of emeralds before that balloon went away."

"I give them hope."

"You sell them lies. You could make an honest living, I'm sure. Instead you fill their heads with pixie dust."

The doctor swiveled to her and made a little bow. He'd been waiting a long time for just this conversation to start.

"You would be surprised at how few dissatisfied customers I have, I think. I figure out what people need to hear and I say it. Does the exhausted farmer's wife need to hear that she has not wasted her life or her talent raising her children and working her land? I tell her she is loved in ways she has yet to notice. And then she looks for these ways. And she comes back to tell me she has found them. And I give her a bottle of Dr. Morgan's Magical Elixir at half price to celebrate."

"And you still make one hundred percent profit on the dose, I'm sure." Jennie put hour glass down.

"So then we're both of us happy. And if you're convinced all I sell are tricks, at least they are good tricks. I think it's far better to use your tricks to make people happy than to use them to make yourself sad."

Jennie cast a look of suspicion at the doctor. "What is that supposed to mean?"

"I tell them stories which at the worst are harmless and at the best are therapy like no doctor can provide. I take nothing from them that they don't willingly give. They come sad, and they leave happy or excited or thoughtful."

"You really think you make them happy with your empty words?"

The doctor paused before replying, "how is what I do different from dancing?"

"I don't dance anymore."

"But you remember how happy you were when you did, and how happy you made everyone who watched you do it. They still tell the story all over the county of the prima donna who would have made Potawatomie county the most famous county in Kansas."

Jennie's expression softened as she stared at the doctor. "They do?"

"It's a sad story," he said. "At least it has a sad ending, assuming, of course, that it has ended. It's the tragic story of a great talent what was never allowed to bloom."

"Leaving a bitter old woman behind, I suppose. People are always resentful of people who have things that they do not have. If I protect my land and my name..." she paused and dropped the sentence. She was working herself up into a passion.

"But that's not how they tell the story at all," said the doctor. "It is the story of sad woman who still dreams of dancing."

"And just how do they know my dreams?"

"It's a story," he said, "and in it the sad woman becomes melancholy but also somehow happy when she hears a waltz on the radio. And she imagines herself dancing, right there in her salon. But she does not dance except in her head. It's the story of a woman who never gave up on dancing, though she no longer dances."

"It's a dumb story," she said.

The doctor had more to say, but a Winkie guard came into the room to tell them they were wanted by the tree. Several monkeys followed them out to the courtyard.

The tree told them that the bubble had landed at the Emerald City and that Glinda the Good, whose bubble it was, had spoken to the Scarecrow and his friends, and that they were on the way and bringing the witch's two-wheeled contraption with them.

"My bike," Jennie said. "I need that back."

Those words or the commanding sound in which she spoke them blew through the gaggle of monkeys like a stiff wind. They hopped like bubbles in boiling water the moment they were spoken, screeching and chattering in a monkey puddle around the one with the golden cap. And then all at once they took to the air. They circled in tight formation and like a storm cloud soared into the sky and away from the castle.

"Good riddance," Jennie said.

13

The monkeys came screaming out of the sky.

They'd seen this before. And just as before, there was no place to hide.

"But didn't they abandon the castle when the witch melted?" the Tin Man cried.

"Get your ax ready for a fight," said the Lion. The Lion remembered trying to outrun the monkeys the last time they had attacked. He had an impulse to try that again. But he fought it. He stood his ground. Running from danger may be more prudent than cowardly, but he was the brawn in this company of brains, brawn, heart, and dog, was he not? And they needed him.

Besides, running hadn't helped at all the last time the monkeys attacked.

"I don't want to hurt them," said the Tin Man, raising his ax.

"You don't want to be dropped from a great height onto jagged rocks either," said the Scarecrow.

Toto stood up in the basket and barked.

The Scarecrow knew from bitter experience that the best he could do to oppose a winged monkey would be of no effect at all. He pulled the bike behind a tree to obscure it, then he flattened himself on the ground and hoped they would not notice he was there.

Leaves and needles rose up into the air like little clouds from the beating of their wings as the monkeys neared the ground. Three monkeys drew the Tin Man in one direction. Three more drew the

Lion in another. No one bothered the Scarecrow. Four grabbed the bike with Toto still in the basket and hoisted it into the air while dozens circled swiftly overhead.

In a moment they were gone.

The Tin Man, Lion, and Scarecrow gathered together and stared up at the flying bike.

"Well that actually went better than expected," said the Lion.

14

If what the tree said was true, there were a lot of crazy things in Oz: not just talking trees and monkeys with wings, but a living scarecrow, and a man made of tin, a talking lion, and a woman who floated in a soap bubble. Jennie was astonished by all of it. But nothing astonished her more than to feel tears rise when she watched four of those horrid, sharp-toothed, flying monkeys softly set her own bicycle down on the courtyard floor near the crabby fruit tree.

Now, why would *that* be astonishing? Why would she almost cry to see her old bike float back to her out of the blue? She wasn't particularly fond of her bike. It just took her places faster than her feet. It was just a practical mode of transportation, nothing more. So why would she almost cry? Why would actual tears rise in her eyes so that she had to scowl to push them back down?

She could not say. Perhaps it was just that the bike was from *home*, from Kansas. Perhaps it was proof to her dream-rattled brain that Kansas still existed somewhere and that this nightmare of a place might not be destined to be her prison forever. Or perhaps it was something about the gesture of the monkeys, whom she'd done nothing to endear to her, flying away, at a mere suggestion, just to please her, the way some people's dogs knew before their owners asked them what they wanted fetched and who they wanted to be kept safe from.

She couldn't explain it, but she couldn't deny that she was moved by the gesture. She released her scowl, and she waltzed over to the bike and grabbed the handle bars in one hand and the seat in the other, and she smiled down on it as though it were her favorite thing in all the world. And she didn't care who saw her do it either.

And that's when Toto popped out of the basket, wagged his tail, and licked her hand.

She pulled back as though she'd been bitten. But she didn't let go of the bike. She didn't let if fall. And she didn't put her scowl back on either. In fact she smiled. She put her hand on Toto's head and brushed it twice, vigorously.

"Decided not to bite me, then?" she said.

Toto put his front paws on the seat and wagged his tail.

"Somebody, come get this dog."

One of the monkeys lifted Toto from the basket.

"What should they do with him?" the doctor asked.

"Just put it down. But keep it away from me. I wouldn't want it to get…" but she paused and changed the direction of her sentence, "to get under my tires."

"That's hopefully thoughtful of you," the doctor said.

"I have to test this thing out. Wouldn't want him, wouldn't want *it* to knock me off."

"Oh, I see."

"Besides he might get hurt."

The bike didn't work.

The chain had come off and gotten wedged between the cog and the frame, and one of the teeth on the rear cog was bent. Jennie had never fixed a bike before, but she understood how the gizmo worked, and with the help of some implements she found in the kitchen she managed to get the chain unstuck and the tooth straightened. She also got some advice from the doctor and thought she'd put some cooking grease on the chain to take away an annoying squeak.

She had the bike upside down, resting on its handlebars and seat, and she was turning the pedals with her hand as the doctor lifted the pot of the grease and stuck a honey dipper in.

That's when the invasion force came into view.

One of the Winkie guards called down from the top of a turret to let them know that the Scarecrow, the Tin Man and the Cowardly Lion were scaling the outer wall.

"How do you know they are *invading*?" Jennie said, walking over.

"They're scaling the outer wall," the guard repeated, and then he added, "of the castle," as though she had not understood what outer wall was being scaled.

"Guests come in through the door," the doctor said.

"We came in a balloon," Jennie said.

"Oh, I see," the doctor said. "So you're saying it's not *our* castle to begin with."

"It may be theirs for all we know."

"Tut, tut," said the crabby fruit tree. It had been silently overseeing the bike repair for hours. "The Winkies think it is your castle and that he's your prisoner. It's a good arrangement. Don't screw it up."

"Why not?" Jennie asked.

"If they find out differently, you will lose your Winkies," said the tree.

"Who wants Winkies?" Jennie asked.

"Who will guard you if you lose your Winkies?" the doctor said.

"Why do I need guarding?"

"Because the apparent owners are scaling the walls of the castle," said the doctor.

"Now you know very well this is the castle of the former Wicked Witch of the West," the tree said.

"Well someone must have inherited it," Jennie noted.

"And one is a lion and another is carrying an ax," said the Winkie guard still watching over the ramparts.

"Open the door," said Jennie. "Raise the gate and lower the drawbridge. Let the invaders invade."

"What if they mean you harm?" the tree asked.

"I have Winkies," she said.

The tree remembered the lion very well. "He brought death and destruction the last time he was here."

As the castle was high and the way was steep, the tree had plenty of time to tell the story of the time the monkeys brought Dorothy Gale and the Cowardly Lion to the castle.

"Dorothy Gale?" said Jennie when the tree mentioned her name. "Dorothy Gale has been here, in this castle?"

"And also her little dog," said the tree. "Didn't you know? *That* is her little dog. I recognized it at once."

"Who is Dorothy Gale?" The doctor asked. "And how could you and a talking tree in Oz possibly know the same person?"

"She's a girl from Kansas," Jennie said as though that explained something. "The dog too?" Jennie said to the tree. She was puzzled. She ran through every day she'd been here in her mind and could not recall this tree ever mentioning that it had seen this dog before. "Well, that *does* explain something," she said. Toto was just then sitting at her feet with his tongue sticking out in a jolly expression.

"Wait, wait, wait. I'm sorry," said the doctor, "someone else from Kansas has been to Oz, and you know who it was? How is that possible?"

"This *is* her dog," Jennie said as though that made everything clear. "And we know she flew away in a house. Surely you heard of that."

"Oh, yes, yes. I did hear that story. A girl and her dog. *This* dog. So Toto *has* been here before," he laughed.

"It wouldn't have been possible without the dog," said the tree. "He's the hero, from a certain point of view, though not mine."

Jennie sat down on a low wall and the hero climbed onto her lap. She did not try to stop him. In fact she hardly seemed to notice he was there at all until she laid her hand on his back as the tree continued with the story right up to the point where the witch melted when Dorothy splashed her with water.

"Oh, let them in," said Jennie when the tree finished. But by then it was too late to let them in. Toto had run to the edge of the ramparts and was barking down at his three friends, who were so close to the top of the wall that it would have meant a lot more work to climb down in order to go in through the gate. A moment later, they were inside, facing down the Winkies.

The Lion roared, the Tin Man, his knees shaking, raised his ax, and the Scarecrow grabbed a bucket of water.

Jennie walked directly up to the Scarecrow, who, standing in the middle, seemed to be the leader. Toto followed step for step.

"What do you want?" she said.

"Douse her," said the Lion.

Toto barked.

"Not until she gives me reason," said the Scarecrow.

"Where is Dorothy?" the Tin Man asked.

"Does everyone know that girl?" The doctor asked.

"I think they do," said Jennie.

"Oh," said the doctor for the second time, "well, that explains the statue. This tree told me there is a statue of a dog like this dog and a little girl in a little town to the east. She must be known all over this place. I don't know how it is I've never met her."

"She's not famous in Kansas," Jennie said. Then she turned back to the invaders. "And that is where she is—Kansas. She did not come with us. So you can put down your weapons—and your bucket of water."

"Don't listen to her," said the Lion. "She's trying to trick you."

Jennie took another step toward the Scarecrow. He raised the bucket ominously. "Let me see that water."

He lowered it. She stuck her hand in the bucket. Everyone gasped. She pulled her hand out unharmed.

"She's more powerful than her sister," said the Tin Man.

"Have you any other business here?" Jennie asked.

"We've come to rescue the Wizard," the Scarecrow said. "We will trade you that wheeled flying machine for him."

"What flying machine?" the doctor asked.

"The two-wheeled broomstick," the Tin Man said.

"Oh, the bike. This bike," the doctor walked over to the bike which was still sitting on its seat and handlebars. "We were just greasing the chain." He turned the pedals to demonstrate.

"Oh, look," said the Tin Man. "We had it upside down."

"So that's what those things are for. I disliked the way they kept bumping into my legs until we fixed that metal rope."

Toto barked.

"They put a tear in my leg," the Scarecrow said.

"Those little rectangles are the handles," said the Tin Man. "Look how he turns the wheel. And look what the metal rope is for." The Tin Man lowered his ax and went over to the doctor. "I do wish I'd brought my oil can."

The Lion walked over as well. "And look. What we thought were handles is a stand."

The Scarecrow and Jennie joined them. "Oh, rapture," said the Scarecrow. "So really there are no other pieces. It stands up on its own."

"But then where do you sit to fly it?" the Lion asked.

"You don't fly it," said Jennie. "You ride it. I'll show you."

The doctor turned the bike over and Jennie climbed onto the seat and pedaled around the courtyard. The monkey with the Golden cap launched himself into the air, and three more monkeys followed. They circled above the bike like a pet cloud as it turned about the courtyard. But by then everyone had been with the monkeys long enough that no one paid them any attention.

"Well that *is* magic," said the Scarecrow, removing his hat to rub his head.

"Why doesn't it fall down?" said the Tin Man.

"When does it take off," asked the Lion.

"And where is the Wizard?"

15

"You're not the Wizard," the Scarecrow said.

"I may not be *the* Wizard," said the doctor, "but that doesn't mean I'm not *a* wizard."

"Are you one the brother wizards?" the Scarecrow asked.

"Do you want us to rescue you?" the Tin Man asked.

"What would you be rescuing me from?"

"The witch's sister," said the Lion. "If we do it before she takes off, we might have a chance."

The doctor seemed to weigh the offer. "I fear what would happen if you rescued me," he said at last, "unless you can rescue both of us."

"You want us to rescue the witch?" the Lion said.

"Call it what you want, we'd be very pleased if you could find a way to return us to Kansas."

"Kansas must be a wonderful place," the Tin Man said. "Everyone seems to be very anxious to leave Oz to get there."

"I've always believed Oz was a wonderful place," said the Scarecrow. "But I suppose unless you have been to other places, you really have no way to know."

"Oz must be very drab and dull compared to a place like Kansas, or else why would everyone want to leave as soon as they arrive?" the Lion asked.

"I wonder," said the doctor.

Jennie finished one last loop of the courtyard and peddled over. The monkeys alighted like pigeons beside her.

"It never took off," said the Lion.

"It doesn't fly," she said.

"At least not without a balloon," said the doctor.

"Ah, but we have the balloon," said the Scarecrow.

"Is that the only way to get out of here?" Jennie sounded more defeated than the doctor thought it was possible for such a woman to sound.

"You don't like balloons?" the Tin Man asked.

"I thought I would catch my death of cold."

"Well there's always the shoes," said the Lion.

"That is how Dorothy went back to Kansas," said the Tin Man.

So they told her the story about the shoes.

"Oh, yes, we've heard of that Glinda," the doctor said.

"Where are these shoes?" Jennie asked.

"Dorothy was wearing them when she left," the Tin Man said. "They're gone."

"Really?" the doctor said.

"Why do you say 'really' like that?" the Scarecrow asked.

"The tree told me that there is a pair of sparkling shoes in the basket of that statue in the east."

"What statue?" Jennie asked.

The tree that had stood as though sleeping since finishing its story shook its leaves: "In the center of Munchkin Land."

The Tin Man hoisted his ax and walked over to the tree and asked about the statue.

"The Munchkins erected a statue for the girl who saved them from this one's sister. It is just a statue of a girl and a dog. And on the front is a plaque that reads:

In Honor of Dorothy Gale
Good Witch of Kansas
Who Bravely Battled
And Soundly Defeated
The Wicked Witch of the East
Freeing All the Munchkins of Oz
From her Tyrannous Tyranny

"Well, I'll be," said the doctor.

"You'll be what?" said the Scarecrow.

"Those shoes can't be real," Jennie said. "Why would you put real shoes in the basket of a statue?"

"This *is* Oz," the doctor reminded her.

"I'm sure they're just bronze with a coat of paint on them."

"I cannot say," said the tree.

"I wish we had a way to know," Jennie said.

"Munchkin Land is clear on the other side of Oz," said the Scarecrow. "Unless you can fly..."

The monkey with the golden cap chattered in the direction of three other monkeys who were there with him. One of them flew off. Looking left and right, two of them grabbed Jennie by the arms and flew her screaming up to the bridge overlooking the courtyard. Toto chased after, and another monkey grabbed him. The others, including half a dozen Winkie guards, ran after the monkeys as quickly as they could, the Lion taking up the rear. But they were too late. The monkey that had flow off first stood on the bridge with a broomstick and a basket. The two monkeys dropped Jennie onto the broomstick and dropped Toto into the basket whose handle they threaded over the broomstick's shaft so that it dangled below. Then they grabbed the broom front and back and hauled it into the air while the frightened woman hung on. In a moment, they were out of sight.

16

Jennie was too stunned to speak. But by the time they cleared the castle and she found herself high over the mountains and trees, she'd recovered enough to say a thing or two. "Where are you taking me?"

"To Munchkin Land," said the monkey with the cap.

And then she was stunned a second time. "You can speak?" she finally said.

"Of course we can speak," said the monkey leader.

"Why haven't you spoken before?"

"You haven't asked me a question before. It's not as though I want to speak to you. I do as you bid because I must."

She thought of other questions she'd like to ask but she was much more concerned about not falling off the broom to bring them up.

"Will this take long?" she asked.

"Yes," the monkey said.

And he was right. Although she did get used to sitting on the shaft of a broomstick pretty quickly, and soon felt safe from falling, she had to shift her weight many times as they crossed over the beautiful Land of Oz to maintain the circulation in her legs. Still, she eventually grew so comfortable, she even dared to stand with one foot on the brush end and one on the shaft because the monkeys promised they would not let her fall. (She felt funny trusting them, but if they were going to drop her or let her fall, they'd have done so by then.) She imagined she was a showman or an acrobat on the wings of a bi-plane at a county fair. She was having so much fun, she danced a step. But a twinge in her knee made her sit down again.

Down below, the land was brilliantly colored, yellow and red, and purple and blue, as though each part of the land were a sectioned off part of a game board. And there was a large green splotch in the middle and yellow lines that must be those roads they'd been talking about radiating out from that center and going everywhere. There was farmland and forest and there were lakes and valleys and mountains. And the whole land was outlined in a beige-colored ribbon. She wondered what mind could have ordered such a large piece of land—it must be larger than all of Kansas and Missouri combined—and done so oh, so cleverly. Would it be possible to do something like that in Kansas?

Eventually she grew bored with sitting and frustrated with the cranky, untalkative monkeys, but she never grew tired of following the natural courses the rivers took against the deliberate patterns of bright yellow road. From this height she could not smell the land, but she imagined the odors of colorful flowers and rich country dirt wafting upwards the way you can sometimes imagine a smell when you look at a beautiful painting. The air up high was cold—although not as cold as it had felt in the balloon, as though some sort of magic from the ground warmed the air even at this height—but she could imagine the warmth of the fields in the yellow land and the cool of the mountain lakes in the blue country. (They were evidently headed toward the blue country.)

Eventually Toto popped his head out of the basket and she picked him up and held him and stopped him from trembling.

At one point it occurred to her that the monkeys could have gone to investigate the shoes without her and to bring them back if they really were the shoes that Dorothy had worn. But when she said this aloud, the monkey with the golden cap did not reply. So she put it in the form of a question.

"Why didn't you just go get the shoes without me?"

"It would have required too much conversation," he said.

She thought that was odd and probably not true. But by then they were so close to the blue land that it wasn't worth discussing.

"Could you fly me all the way to Kansas?" she asked.

"No," the monkey said.

She breathed out a puff of exasperation. But no one noticed.

These infuriatingly curt answers reminded her of the way Claire reacted when she told her she would not be sending her to the arts academy to learn to paint—that she would not let her waste her time, and that she herself would not waste money on such trivial things. Clipped little one-word answers were not kind or proper in Claire and they were not kind or helpful in the mouth of this obnoxious monkey. When Claire had spoken to her that way, she was quick to tell her she had money to send her to a real school where she could learn about real things, like farming and business and law and government, and that was all the money she had. But that hadn't helped at all.

The broomstick descended at last on a brightly colored square with a pond and a river of blue water. All around it were houses, little and round, with thatched roofs—all but one. That one house appeared to be a farmhouse, the kind you see all over Kansas, with white clapboard sides and gables and a chimney and a little covered entranceway. It was really out of place in color and style as though it had been dropped in where it didn't belong. It even appeared to be a little broken as if it actually had been dropped in.

So that must be the Gale farmhouse. Had a cyclone really carried the house all this way? She couldn't imagine it.

As they approached the ground, out of all the little houses the residents of this little town flowed like ants from a damaged anthill, wearing identical blue clothes. Some stopped and looked up and pointed and shouted. Some ran across the square and pounded on the doors of buildings. And they filled the air with noise. By the time Jennie and the broom settled down beside a pond the whole town was abustle with clamor and confusion. It reminded her of that town meeting in the Wamego High School gym when the good governor of Kansas came to rail against the crazy men in Washington who said they were going to fix all the nation's problems by paying Kansas farmers *not to work*.

"Excuse me," she yelled now as she'd yelled then. But the people kept running and clambering. She tried to calm them down as she'd tried to calm down the Kansas farmers to get them to listen to the governor's sensible proposals. "We're just..."

But they just did not listen.

Then she noticed how remarkably small they all were. They were really little people, no bigger than children, although they did not appear to be children.

"Will the things in this Land of Oz ever stop astonishing me?" she said aloud.

"No," said the monkey at her side.

"Never mind these little people," she said. "Just bring me those shoes if they are not made of bronze." She pointed to the little statue of Dorothy and Toto that stood between the pond and the fence that ran along the river.

The monkey made a move toward the statue. And as soon as he did, crowds of little people filled the space between her and it, and the monkey could not pass. He leapt into the air in order to swoop down on the shoes. But before he could reach for them, one of the little people plucked them from the basket. And she passed them to another person, who passed one left and the other right and all the monkeys took to the air and tried to follow the shoes as they passed through the crowd, but the monkeys soon became confused and the shoes were hopelessly lost somewhere among the giggling multitude.

That's when Toto took on the challenge. He scooted among the legs of the little people barking and yapping and sniffing the air. The Munchkins danced out of his way as though he were coming for them. But he did not slow down. He pressed his forepaws against the legs of one Munchkin after another and barked up at their faces and sniffed. He snaked around one and then another as though he were running an obstacle course.

Meanwhile, the monkey with the golden cap lighted on one of the pillars of the fence, scanned the churning crowd, and hissed. Everyone cringed.

"I need those shoes," Jennie called over the heads of the people.

And then one brave little woman in a deep blue coat came forward and said, half out of breath, "You will not get them this time."

"I must have them," Jennie repeated.

And another little person joined the first one. "We will not let you rule here anymore. No more wicked witches."

The crowd of Munchkins flowed back and forth like a turbulent sea under the wild rampage of the little dog.

"I've seen the bravery of tiny people before," Jennie said.

A monkey floated from the pillar of the bridge at the sighting of a sparkle and headed for a Munchkin girl who just managed to pass the shoe to another as the monkey swooped in and swiped at the air.

"We may be small, but we are many," said a third from the crowd. "Together we are more powerful than you. So you might as well take your monkeys and leave."

"You cannot hide those shoes all night," Jennie yelled.

Toto stopped and panted.

"Your beast cannot attack us all night," said a chubby Munchkin in a long blue overcoat.

Toto looked around, sniffed the air, and charged again.

"If you don't give me the shoes, my monkeys will grab you two at a time and carry you away."

"They're going to drop us in the desert," said one.

"They're going to fly us to the Nome King," said another.

And the whole crowd took a step back.

"Could be," Jennie replied as though she knew what they were talking about, "if you don't hand over my shoes."

And a gasp ran through the crowd.

"No," said an important-looking Munchkin to the crowd. "Monkeys or no monkeys, she will not get the shoes. You think she has power now, remember what her sister did when she wore the shoes. We are more powerful than she, and she will not get the shoes."

Just then Toto leapt at a flash of light and grabbed a shoe in his mouth as it passed from one hand to another, and he darted with it to Jennie who took it and held it in triumph.

"Get that shoe back," the Munchkin girl ordered.

Three Munchkins charged Jennie, but Jennie, still holding her broomstick, easily sashayed away, and started laughing. "One more to go," she laughed.

Then half a dozen other Munchkins came forward, and she danced away again, swinging the broom and holding the shoe high over her head where no one could reach it.

"I'm a-going home," she sang as she danced with her broom. "Kansas, I'm a-going home." She appeared almost to be breaking into song as she danced along the landing by the pond like a toreador. And the Munchkins charged again in greater numbers and she wiggled her hips and spun around and made them miss and a number of them overshot and landed in the water. She was having fun. Toto ran around her feet, barking, keeping the Munchkins away.

She felt a twinge her in knee. She hesitated a moment in her foray, and then one Munchkin managed to grab her skirt on her left. And another grabbed her skirt on her right. Another one caught hold of the brush of her broom. And in a moment half a dozen Munchkins were holding her still. One Munchkin climbed the back of another to reach up to the elevated shoe.

But she did not panic. She hurled the shoe in air as far as she could. And the monkey with the golden cap caught it at the highest point of its arc and carried it well above the crowd.

And all the Munchkins let her go.

"We still need one more shoe," she yelled.

The crowd sighed and then went quiet.

Everyone's attention turned to the giant soap bubble descending on the square. Jennie stared at the many-colored bubble as it grew until it was as large as she was. And then it popped. And there before everyone stood the woman in white she'd heard of from the Scarecrow and the tree, her white hat an exact match for Jennie's black one.

"Glinda," she said, not loud enough for anyone to hear.

The little people drew aside to let the sorceress pass; she went directly up the steps and looked Jennie in the eyes. "So you are the sister of the Witch of the East and the Witch of the West. How is it I've never heard of you?"

"I am nobody's sister," Jennie said.

"But you are a witch." Glinda touched the broomstick in Jennie's hand with the starburst at the end of her wand.

"You are not the first person to call me that."

Jennie would not have let herself appear frightened of the sorceress even if she were frightened. But she was glad to realize that she was not at all scared of the woman, whatever her powers might be. Perhaps that is because she had dealt with a lot of powerful people through the years who had tried to intimidate her. Or maybe it was that this woman really did not seem to be trying to intimidate her. She was just talking to her as though all she really wanted was information. In fact Glinda seemed almost friendly.

"But I am not a witch," Jennie continued. "I follow the law, and I take what is mine. That does not make me a witch."

"The shoes are not yours," Glinda said.

Jennie raised a hand to her chin. That detail had not occurred to her. She needed the shoes. She might never get home without them. So how could they not be hers?

"But I have to have them," she said.

"They belong to the Munchkins," Glinda said. "You cannot have them. Or if you thought you could, this is not the way to get them. I doubt they'll ever give them to you now."

Jennie bit her lip. "Are you saying there was another way to get the shoes?" If there was, she had no idea what it might be.

"Not now," said Glinda. "So you might as well hop on your broom and leave."

"But I have one shoe already," she said.

Glinda held out her hand. The shoe the monkey had grabbed was in it. The monkey headed back to the pillar of the fence.

"You can do nothing here. It is time for you and your broomstick to leave." Glinda's tone remained friendly. There was no hint of anger or even of challenge in her voice. She seemed even a little sorry to have to say it. But she was no more intimidated by Jennie than Jennie was of her.

Jennie was outmaneuvered. She had been outmaneuvered before, but not often and not for a long time. She'd almost always found a way to win even when she'd lost. But she could not see any way now. And this was the biggest loss she'd ever suffered. She'd lost her home. And Claire. She did not want to risk going over an ocean again in a balloon even if she could get one. Who knew where a balloon would take her? No, the only chance she had to really get home was the shoes.

But she didn't bow her head. She did not plead. She did not ask to start over. She was proud and composed. She might be defeated but she would never appear so. She stared at the crowd of silent, watchful Munchkins.

Glinda waited.

Toto barked. And that was the first time Glinda noticed the dog, standing beside Jennie, wagging his tail and panting.

"Toto?" she said.

Toto barked again. Another gasp went through the crowd. "Is that really Toto? Then where is Dorothy?"

"Dorothy is in Kansas."

"Toto, are you with the witch?"

Toto barked and put his paws on Jennie's legs so that she picked him up. In her arms, he barked and wagged his tail.

"Oh, dear," said Glinda. "I'm afraid I'm a little baffled. Are you a *friend* of Dorothy?" Glinda's friendly tone became even friendlier.

It occurred to Jennie that she should say she was a friend of Dorothy. But she could not bring herself to say so, not even to get the shoes. She could not say why.

What she said instead was, "I'm a friend of Toto's." And Toto licked her face and barked at Glinda. "And I want to go home."

"Is that the *only* reason you want the shoes?" Glinda asked.

"What else do they do?"

"Never mind," the sorceress said. "What do you think, Toto?"

Toto yipped and wagged.

Glinda turned to the crowd of anxious Munchkins. "Friends, I now think things are not as they appear. This woman is not a *wicked* witch. She may not be a witch at all. She's a harmless humbug pretending to be a witch."

Jennie summoned all her strength not to respond.

"Shall we let her borrow the shoes?"

A murmur went through the crowd.

The important-looking Munchkin stood on the landing and called for the missing shoe, which was presented to her in a moment. Then, walking in a dignified way, she received the other shoe from Glinda's hand, and presented the pair to Jennie.

"Why didn't you just ask for them in the first place?"

Jennie didn't know what to say. She wanted to say, "because I didn't think you'd give them to me." But the truth was it had never occurred to her to *ask* for them. So she just said, "I am very grateful. Thank you all. I'm sorry."

"How wonderful," Glinda said. "Now off with you."

And she was going to ask how, but she remembered the Scarecrow had already told her how Dorothy had used the shoes to get home. So she said, "Will they work for the doctor and Toto as well?"

"The doctor? You mean the wizard."

"The wizard? Why does everyone think he's a wizard?"

"They will work for anyone," Glinda said. "You need to have Toto in your arms and you need to hold the wizard's hand as you say the spell and perform the magic."

"That's all?"

"That's all."

17

The doctor tried to explain how gyroscopic forces worked. But not even the Scarecrow's marvelous brain could understand.

"You must be wiser than the Wizard to know about such things," they said.

"I couldn't say, but it's really not all that difficult. Anyone can ride a bike."

"So the magic is in the bike," said the Scarecrow.

"Yes, I see. The bike is magic," the Tin Man said, putting his hand to his chest. "Now it all makes sense."

The doctor looked away a moment, then he put a hand on the shoulder of the Scarecrow and a hand on the shoulder of the Tin Man. "Yes," he said, "it's magic."

"Ah, well that *does* make sense," said the Lion, backing up a step.

"The magic is in the machine, so to speak, not the rider. That's why anyone can do it," the doctor said. And he showed him first by riding the bike himself, then teaching the Tin Man and then the reluctant Lion. The Scarecrow never did learn to ride the bike because he could not push the pedals hard enough with the straw in his legs. And so the doctor had to change his mind, "Well, *most* of the magic is in the machine. Some of it is in the rider." And then he taught a few of the Winkie guards the trick as well.

"Such marvelous things as these would be useful in the Land of Oz," said the Lion. "What a lovely way to get from one place to another."

"I don't imagine they are too hard to make," he said, "if you have one to copy."

"But who will put the magic in?" said the Scarecrow.

The doctor was still thinking of an answer when the winged monkeys dropped Jennie back among them.

She was talking to the one that wore the golden cap.

"So why do you do what I ask you to?"

"Because you have the golden cap. We must obey," the monkey said.

"They talk?" said the doctor.

"Only if you ask them a direct question," said Jennie.

"Why do you only answer direct questions," the doctor asked the nearest monkey. But he got no answer.

"Oh, and they only talk to me," Jennie informed the doctor. "Why is that?" she asked the monkey.

"*You* have the hat," said the monkey.

"The hat? What hat?" she was wearing the hat she always wore, the tall, pointed one she'd found in the kitchen. She took it off and showed it to the monkey as though to prove that it was not made of gold and that there was no other hat underneath.

"*You* have the golden cap." She pointed to the hat on the monkey's head. He raised his hand to touch it. He looked startled. He took it off and turned it over. He screeched once, and all the monkeys in the castle—hundreds of them—hurried to the courtyard. They flew out of every window and poured in over the walls. Jennie's eyes grew large. They must have been clinging to the side of the mountain like bats. She had had no idea how many there were. They filled the courtyard. Still screeching, the lead monkey looked from one to another of his minions jumping and making noise as though he were being pestered by a swarm of bees. He launched himself just above their heads and waved the golden cap at the dark mass of monkeys without pausing his chatter for a moment.

And then he put the cap back on his head, and he took off into the sky. And all the monkeys screamed until everyone's ears hurt, and away they flew after him without looking back or saying goodbye.

"Well, that was rude," said the Lion, taking his hands from his ears.

But Jennie lowered her hands and laughed. She laughed a long and happy laugh like she had not laughed in years. The doctor was astonished to hear it. He would have sworn if he'd thought about it that her dusty old voice was no longer capable of such laughter. She laughed herself almost to tears.

"Well, now we know she's not a witch," said the Scarecrow.

"Save me from ever being as dumb as a monkey," she said, "no offense to monkeys."

The Tin Man gave her a funny look.

"No, they were very helpful to me," Jennie said, "and I won't say a bad word about them. And now I'm afraid we too must leave. I have the shoes. I am told we can leave whenever we want."

"Oh, that's marvelous. Splendid. I'm so anxious to see if my horse is okay." He looked around and raised his hand as though to wave to everyone. He did not see joy on any face. "But, of course, we can't leave like the monkeys did. We must say goodbye properly, like people. And if we can go whenever we want, there is no hurry."

And he ran over to the captain of the Winkie guards and said something to him that no one else could hear. When he heard it, the captain laughed.

"But won't they be glad to see us go? I would think they would be," Jennie said.

The tree grumbled and shook its leaves and said in a booming voice, "I'm sure the Winkie slaves will be happy to see the last wicked witch of Oz leave for good."

"Slaves?" said the captain of the Winkie guards. "Why do you call us slaves?"

"Because we call things by their names," said the tree.

"We are not slaves," the captain walked up to the tree and then turned and faced Jennie and the doctor. "We are guards."

"You came when your mistress returned," said the tree. "You came out of fear to serve your wicked mistress."

"Oh, no," the captain said. "Is that what you thought? We came as guards."

"As guards to a witch," said the tree.

"As guards for the Winkies," said the captain. "We are not here to protect you," he said to Jennie.

"You're not?" said Jennie.

The captain laughed. "We're here to make sure you do not leave the castle."

"But the monkeys," said the doctor.

"Yes, they defeated us," said the captain.

"So you're saying you are actually here to imprison me?"

"We thought you knew. But as you have never been unkind to us and as you are willing to leave Oz altogether, we are happy to let you go. Indeed, as the Wizard has whispered in my ear, we would like to throw you a feast to celebrate, once again, the liberation of Oz."

The captain bowed and a half a dozen of his soldiers marched into the castle along with the doctor. And in less than a minute the doctor came out, with his fiddle in hand.

"I think, while we wait for the Winkies to prepare our farewell feast, we shall hear a little music."

And he cleared his throat and tuned his instrument and launched into an old barnyard tune he'd known for thirty years. Jennie offered no resistance at all. In fact she was so happy that she tapped her foot. And the doctor said, "Dance for us, Jennie." And she blushed, and she went out into the middle of the courtyard, and she danced. She danced with the Lion, and she danced with the Scarecrow and she danced with the Tin Man, and then she danced with the doctor as he played. And she even went up to the crabby tree and invited it to sway—but all it did was sneer and fold its branches like arms. But she just smiled and laughed and turned her back. She skipped into the center of the courtyard, and she did her solo. Her knee was hurting pretty badly by then, but she didn't stop. She was having too much fun. The Winkies who were not in the kitchen all clapped to the beat. And she spun and clicked her heecls. And she did a pirouette and then crossed the stage in three, four, five great leaps, landing always on her good leg. Then she clicked her heels again and spun around. Toto ran up to her and barked. And she picked him up and twirled him like a partner and tossed him in the air and gracefully caught him as she leaped and landed and clicked her heels again and said aloud, "We're going home."

And as she said it, she landed on her injured leg, and she grimaced, and she uttered an aching groan—and she disappeared.

The doctor stopped playing at once. Everyone looked shocked. The happiness dropped from his face.

"Oh, dear," he said.

18

They still had their feast, but it was not as happy as expected.

"People have to eat," said the doctor, "and I guess these Winkies have a long walk home."

"She wasn't so bad," the captain of the guards said, "but I hope that's the last of the sisters,"

"Yes, I think we are done with sisters," the Scarecrow said.

"But her disappearance leaves me in a bit of a bind," the doctor said.

"Well, we still have the balloon," said the Tin Man. "And I even think the Scarecrow knows how it works."

But the Scarecrow had another proposition for the doctor.

"As one of the brother wizards, I wonder if you might want to stay in the Emerald City in your brother's place. You could make your bicycles and rule the great Land of Oz at the same time."

"Why, yes," said the Tin Man. "The Scarecrow has said many times that ruling is not to his liking. There is much in this magical land of ours, that he would prefer to explore."

"I know that must not seem like much of a thing to do for someone who hails from the marvelous land of Kansas, but this is our home, and we are humble people," the Scarecrow added, "and we will be very satisfied to see our own back yard."

The doctor promised to consider it, although in fact, he'd already made up his mind. There wasn't much left for him in Kansas. There wasn't much of real value in his wagon. He didn't even have his struggle with Jennie to look forward to if he went back, as they were friends now, and she probably would allow him to stay in the county, sheriff or no sheriff. He only hoped his horse would be well cared for by whoever claimed it.

Here, in this Land of Oz, he would be hailed as a wizard and perhaps even made an emperor. And he could spend his time talking with the good people of the Emerald City that the Scarecrow and his friends spoke so highly of, and making bicycles. It felt like a pretty good life.

At the same time, he'd keep the balloon, in the unlikely event he ever did feel the pull of Kansas or a push from the good people of Oz. (It wouldn't be the first time he'd felt a push from the good people of one place or another if he did.)

But he didn't accept the offer right away. He thought it best not to appear too eager, lest they suppose he was a humbug.

"I will think of it," he said for a second time.

19

Jennie would never ride a bike again. She did not yet realize that when she landed back in Kansas. But she would find out soon. That last episode of dancing had done it. Her knee would hurt whenever she exerted herself. But she would not mind very much. She wouldn't have traded that afternoon for all of Potawatomie County. She only regretted that she'd somehow made that magic of the shoes work without her arm around the doctor. He must think her an awful witch, she thought, to abandon him like that, although it really was an accident.

Oh, but there was no way to tell him. The shoes did not come with her back to Kansas. (Nor did the black hat. The only thing she'd brought back from that mysterious land was the single emerald that she'd caught when she first spotted the balloon.)

She'd landed barefoot by the side of the road at the very spot where the balloon had taken her away. The doctor's horse was still grazing in the field, the wagon still attached. It was the least she could do, she decided, to bring the horse home to her farm and give it a nice pasture. It really was a fine animal. And anyway, her knee hurt so badly when she landed that she could not possibly have walked home, and it was nice to be able to climb into the wagon and drive it.

She'd have to return Toto of course. And that made her sad. She'd grown very fond of the little dog. And to add to that, she wasn't sure at first how she would get him home. She thought maybe if she just let the dog loose he would find his own way home. But that did not feel right.

She finally decided to ask Claire to help. That would make Claire happy. She was anxious to talk to Claire. There was so much that needed to be said.

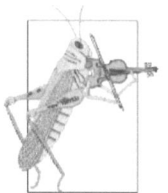

Interset Press is a small, independent press located in Southern New Hampshire. Lacking deep pockets for promotion in the crowded, competitive field of commercial fiction, it relies on word of mouth advertising. If you enjoyed this book, please tell your friends, rate the title on Amazon.com, or put a comment on our Facebook page.

www.ingramcontent.com/pod-product-compliance
Lightning Source LLC
Chambersburg PA
CBHW022039170626
46808CB00003B/1272

* 9 7 8 1 5 7 4 3 3 0 4 9 6 *